A police car stopped in the Brown driveway. Officer Friedman got out, followed by Bugs Meany. The Tiger leader wore a bathing suit and a beautiful suntan.

"Bugs claims you have his watch," said Officer Friedman.

"Don't look so sweet and innocent, Encyclopedia," growled Bugs. "Those two big guys came up on me while I was sunbathing all morning and took the watch right off my wrist. I followed them to the road and saw them give it to you!"

"I was out at the lighthouse all morning," said Encyclopedia.

Bugs strutted around, showing off his tan. "I'll bet this little crook hid my watch right here."

"Search the place," Encyclopedia invited. "You won't find it here."

"Oh, yeah?" sneered Bugs. As he talked his smoothly tanned hands and wrists dipped into the boxes on the top shelf. Suddenly he pulled out the watch. "Here it is!"

"Stop acting, Bugs," said Encyclopedia. "It won't work. Your wristwatch was never stolen."

WHAT WAS ENCYCLOPEDIA'S PROOF?

ENCYCLOPEDIA BROWN
Keeps the Peace

BY DONALD J. SOBOL

Illustrated by
Leonard Shortall

A BANTAM SKYLARK BOOK

For
My Son
John

*This low-priced Bantam Book
has been completely reset in a type face
designed for easy reading, and was printed
from new plates. It contains the complete
text of the original hard-cover edition.*
NOT ONE WORD HAS BEEN OMITTED.

RL 6, IL 5-up

ENCYCLOPEDIA BROWN KEEPS THE PEACE

*A Bantam Skylark Book / published by arrangement with
Thomas Nelson, Inc., Publishers*

PRINTING HISTORY

*Thomas Nelson edition published September 1969
9 printings through 1978*

Bantam Skylark edition / September 1978

2nd printing . . . . . . October 1978	4th printing . . . . July 1979
3rd printing . . . . June 1979	5th printing . . . . . December 1979
6th printing . . . . . . May 1980	

ISBN 0-553-15104-5

Published simultaneously in the United States and Canada

*Bantam Books are published by Bantam Books, Inc. Its trade-
mark, consisting of the words "Bantam Books" and the por-
trayal of a bantam, is Registered in U.S. Patent and Trademark
Office and in other countries. Marca Registrada. Bantam
Books, Inc., 666 Fifth Avenue, New York, New York 10019.*

PRINTED IN THE UNITED STATES OF AMERICA

15 14 13 12 11 10 9 8 7 6

Contents

ENCYCLOPEDIA BROWN
Keeps the Peace

The Case of
the Silver Fruit Bowl

"Stay away from Idaville!"

Across the nation the warning sped from crook to crook.

Big and small, they knew what to expect if they tried anything funny in Idaville—a quick trip to jail. For more than a year, no child or grown-up had gotten away with breaking a law there.

How did Idaville do it? What secret lay behind its war on crime? No one could guess. Idaville looked like many other seaside towns its size.

It had two car washes, two delicatessens, three movie theaters, and four banks. It had rich families and poor families, churches and a synagogue, lovely beaches, and good places to fish.

And on Rover Avenue it had a red brick house with a white picket fence in front.

This was the real headquarters of Idaville's war on crime. For within the red brick walls lived Encyclopedia Brown.

Encyclopedia's father was chief of the Idaville police. For more than a year now Chief Brown had brought home his hardest cases. Encyclopedia solved them at the dinner table.

It pained Chief Brown not to tell the world. He wanted to shout from the rooftops, "My son is the greatest detective who ever walked in sneakers!"

But how could he?

Who would believe that the mastermind behind Idaville's crime cleanup was ten years old?

Encyclopedia never let drop a word about the help he gave his father. He didn't want to seem different from other fifth-graders.

His nickname was something else. There was nothing he could do about *it*.

Only his parents and teachers called him

by his real name, Leroy. Everyone else in Idaville called him Encyclopedia.

An encyclopedia is a book or set of books filled with facts from A to Z. So was Encyclopedia's head. He had read more books than anybody, and he never forgot a word. You might say he was the only library in America that could play second base.

One evening his father ate his soup very slowly. Encyclopedia knew what that meant. Chief Brown had come up against a case he couldn't solve.

Chief Brown put down his spoon. He leaned back and said, "Mr. Holt says he was robbed this afternoon."

"Says?" questioned Mrs. Brown. "You make it sound as if you don't believe him."

"I'm not sure, " replied Chief Brown. "Mr. Holt owns the Silver Shop on Main Street. He claims that eight fine silver dishes were stolen. No one saw the holdup, however."

"Why should he lie?" asked Mrs. Brown.

"Mr. Holt won't lose any money because of the robbery," said Chief Brown. "He doesn't own the silver dishes that were stolen."

"Who owns them?" asked Encyclopedia.

"Mrs. Cartwright," answered Chief Brown. "Mr. Holt agreed to show the dishes in his store. If he sold them at the price Mrs. Cartwright was asking, she was to pay him for his time and trouble."

"Do you think he claimed the dishes were stolen so that he can sell them himself out of town and keep all the money?" asked Encyclopedia.

"It has been done before," said Chief Brown.

"Did Mr. Holt see who held him up?" inquired Mrs. Brown.

"A single gunman," said Chief Brown. "Mr. Holt is sure he can recognize the man if he sees him again."

Chief Brown unbuttoned his shirt pocket. He took out a notebook.

"I wrote down everything Mr. Holt told me about the holdup," he said to Encyclopedia. "Here is what he said happened."

Chief Brown read:

"I was alone in the store shortly after one o'clock. I had my back to the door. I was locking a wall showcase in which I keep

eight very fine silver dishes belonging to Mrs. Cartwright. Suddenly I heard the door open. A man's voice said, 'Don't turn around—this is a stickup!' I felt a gun in my back. 'Just hand over everything in the showcase,' the voice said. After I had given him everything—it sounded as if he put the dishes in a suitcase—he left."

Encyclopedia said, "Mr. Holt's back was to the holdup man all the time. So how can he say he could recognize the man if he saw him again?"

Mrs. Brown looked at Encyclopedia proudly. She was always pleased when he solved a case before she got up to bring the main course.

"Mr. Holt said something else," replied Chief Brown. He read again from his notebook.

"All the silver dishes were highly polished. When I was passing back the largest, a fruit bowl made by Falco of Italy, I tipped it up. By looking inside it, I saw the holdup man's face just as though I were looking into a mirror."

*"I saw the holdup man's face just as though I were
looking into a mirror,"* said Mr. Holt.

Mrs. Brown glanced worriedly at Encyclopedia.

Encyclopedia had closed his eyes. He always closed his eyes when he did his heavy thinking.

Chief Brown put his notebook into his pocket. "It's not such a simple case after all," he said. "I can't be sure that Mr. Holt isn't telling the truth."

Encyclopedia opened his eyes. "Is his business doing well?" he asked.

"No," said Chief Brown. "I checked with his bank. He has borrowed a lot of money to keep the store going. I think he faked the robbery. With the money he will get from selling the silver dishes out of town, he can pay back the bank."

"You aren't being fair," said Mrs. Brown. "Just because Mr. Holt needs money doesn't mean he stole Mrs. Cartwright's silver."

"Have you ever seen the silver bowl he used as a mirror, Dad?" asked Encyclopedia.

"Your mother and I nearly bought the bowl last month, as a matter of fact," said Chief Brown. "It's about eleven inches across and rounded inside like a big spoon."

"We just loved it," said Mrs. Brown. "But it cost too much."

"I'm glad you didn't buy it," said Encyclopedia.

"Why?" asked Chief Brown.

"Because Mr. Holt needed the fruit bowl for his story," said Encyclopedia. "He was afraid he might not get away with a simple story of a holdup man. He had to add something that showed he acted to get back Mrs. Cartwright's silver dishes. So he put in the part about using the fruit bowl as a mirror to see the holdup man's face."

"I'm afraid that part doesn't matter," said Chief Brown. "We can't prove that he didn't see the holdup man's face any more than we can prove he made up the whole story. Maybe there was a holdup man, maybe there wasn't. We're back where we started."

"Not quite, Dad," said Encyclopedia. "We know that Mr. Holt is lying!"

WHAT MADE ENCYCLOPEDIA SURE?

*(Turn to page 73 for the solution to
The Case of the Silver Fruit Bowl.)*

The Case of
the Dwarf's Beard

During the winter Encyclopedia solved cases in the dining room. In the summer he solved them in the garage as well.

When school let out, he opened his own detective business. He wanted to help the children of the neighborhood. Outside the garage each morning he hung a sign. It read:

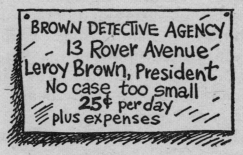

BROWN DETECTIVE AGENCY
13 Rover Avenue
Leroy Brown, President
No case too small
25¢ per day
plus expenses

One morning Gary Hale brought in a beer can. The bottom was missing.

"Look at this," exclaimed Gary.

He poked his thumb through a hole in the side of the can.

"The hole is for air," said Gary. "Bugs Meany made it before he stuck the can over my dwarf."

Encyclopedia stayed calm. He tried to recall the last time anyone had stuck a beer can over a dwarf. Only Bugs Meany would do such a thing.

Bugs was the leader of a gang of tough older boys who called themselves the Tigers. They should have called themselves the Tea Bags. They were always getting into hot water.

"I want to hire you," said Gary, putting twenty-five cents on the gasoline can beside Encyclopedia. "Somebody's got to stop that Bugs Meany, and I'm too small."

"I think I can handle Bugs," said Encyclopedia. Since opening his detective agency, Encyclopedia had been hired to stop many of Bugs's shady deals. "What are the facts?"

"Did you know about Mr. Whitten's jelly-bean contest?" asked Gary.

"Sure. Children had to guess the number of jelly beans in the window of his toy shop."

"My guess was closest," said Gary. "But I'm not proud of winning."

"Is Mr. Whitten your uncle or something?"

"No," said Gary. "My guess was honest—seven thousand and twenty-three jelly beans. The real number was eleven thousand and six. My guess was closest, so I won. But I looked bad."

"It hurt your standing to miss by so much," said Encyclopedia sympathetically.

"Right," said Gary, whose hobby was entering contests.

So far this year Gary had finished eighty-first in a national TV hair-tonic contest, winning two free shaves at a barbershop in Denver, Colorado. He had also won a year's subscription to *The Hardware Store News* and many smaller prizes.

"First prize in the jelly-bean contest was seven candles shaped like Snow White's dwarfs," said Gary. "Last night I picked up the candles at Mr. Whitten's shop. I'd hardly got out the door before Bugs Meany and his Tigers took them away."

"What did you do?"

"Nothing," said Gary. "I told you, I'm too little. But I followed the Tigers to the highway. They used a candle to light firecrackers. When a firecracker went off, it sounded like a tire blew. Cars were stopping all over the place."

"What about the empty beer can?"

"There was a strong breeze," answered Gary. "Bugs Meany put the beer can over the candle so it wouldn't go out. He lighted the firecrackers through the hole in the side."

"Hmmm," said Encyclopedia. "We better pay Bugs a visit."

The Tigers' clubhouse was an unused tool shed behind Mr. Sweeny's Auto Body Shop. Bugs Meany was alone. He had a deck of playing cards and was marking the backs of the aces and kings.

"Get off the earth," he snarled upon seeing the boy detective, "or I'll twist your nose so far around you'll part your hair every time you sneeze."

Encyclopedia was used to Bugs's welcomes. He stepped inside. Immediately his

*Bugs Meany had a deck of playing cards and was
marking the backs of the aces and kings.*

gaze fell upon an object standing on an orange crate.

It was a candle shaped like a dwarf!

Although the head had melted away, Encyclopedia could tell that the front of the dwarf faced the door. All the drippings had slid down the chest and legs, forming a beard clear to the little wax boots.

"That's one of the candles you stole from Gary last night," said Encyclopedia. "He won seven of them in Mr. Whitten's jelly-bean-counting contest."

"You've got bubbles in your think tank," jeered Bugs. "If I had nothing better to do than enter contests, I'd go jump in the lake."

"You used one of my candles to light firecrackers by the highway last night," said Gary.

"Man, oh, man!" sang Bugs. "I'm accused of everything! I bought that candle two days ago and put it there on the orange crate. I haven't touched it since!"

"How come it's burned down," demanded Gary.

"I said I didn't *touch* it," replied Bugs. "I didn't say I didn't *light* it. I lit it last night to show the other Tigers I was in the club-house."

"They couldn't see the light. The club-house has no windows," pointed out Encyclopedia.

"What I put up with!" groaned Bugs, rolling his eyes. "I left the door open, you blubberbrain!"

"There was a strong breeze last night," said Encyclopedia. "It probably would have blown out the candle."

For a moment Bugs looked as if he'd taken a karate chop to the throat.

"W-well, the breeze wasn't strong *enough*," he insisted. "You can see the candle burned pretty well."

"Too well," corrected Encyclopedia.

WHAT DID ENCYCLOPEDIA MEAN?

*(Turn to page 74 for the solution to
The Case of the Dwarf's Beard.)*

The Case of
Bugs Meany's Revenge

The world of Bugs Meany was divided in two.

One half was filled with mischief. The other was filled with the desire to get even with Encyclopedia.

Bugs hated having Encyclopedia outsmart him all the time. He longed to knock the boy detective colder than the paint on an icehouse floor, and twice as flat.

Bugs didn't dare throw a punch, however. It wasn't because Encyclopedia's father was chief of police. It was because of Sally Kimball.

Bugs had never dreamed that a pretty ten-year-old *girl* could beat the ground with him—till Sally had caught him bullying a Cub Scout.

Bugs had laughed when Sally had told him to pick on someone his own size. He had roared in surprise when she had dropped him with her first punch. He had gotten up, but after she had served him a helping of lefts and rights, he had just lain on the grass and groaned.

Because of Sally, Bugs never threatened Encyclopedia with his muscles. Sally was the boy detective's junior partner.

"Bugs hates me, and he won't ever live down the licking you gave him," warned Encyclopedia.

"We'd better keep on our guard," agreed Sally. "He's like a spinning restaurant—always trying to turn the tables."

"I suppose we ought to thank him," said Encyclopedia. "His troublemaking brings in business."

"That reminds me," said Sally. "I came by around noon and saw Duke Kelly, one of Bugs's Tigers, stealing out of the detective agency. Where were you?"

"Out," said Encyclopedia. "I received a telephone call from a boy who called himself Mike Gaither," said Encyclopedia. "He asked me to meet him out by the old lighthouse right away. I waited there an hour. He never showed up."

"A phony telephone call. . . . Then, while you were gone, Duke Kelly. . . ." Sally frowned. "I smell Bugs Meany!"

"I doubt that Bugs will bother us for a while," said Encyclopedia. "He's too busy building himself into Mr. Junior Idaville."

"Mr. Junior Idaville?" asked Sally.

"The Y.M.C.A. is holding a body-building contest next week," said Encyclopedia. "The man with the best build will be crowned Mr. Idaville. The title Mr. Junior Idaville will go to the boy with the biggest muscles."

"If Bugs takes off his hat, he's a cinch to win," said Sally.

Just then a police car stopped in the Brown driveway. Officer Friedman got out, followed by Bugs Meany. The Tiger leader wore a bathing suit and a beautiful suntan.

"I've said all summer this detective business isn't on the level. It's just a front

Officer Friedman got out, followed by Bugs Meany in a bathing suit and a beautiful suntan.

for passing stolen goods!" exclaimed Bugs.

"Cool off, Bugs," said Officer Friedman. And to Encyclopedia he said, "Bugs claims you have his wristwatch."

"I don't know what you're talking about," said Encyclopedia.

"Oh, yes you do!" bellowed Bugs. "Those two gorillas gave it to you!"

"Huh!" said Encyclopedia.

"Don't look so sweet and innocent," growled Bugs. "Those two big guys came up on me while I was lying on the beach at noon today. They took the watch right off my wrist. I followed them to the road. I saw them give the watch to you."

"Where were you at noon today?" Officer Friedman asked Encyclopedia.

"I was out at the old lighthouse," answered Encyclopedia, and he explained about the mysterious telephone call.

"Did anyone see you at the lighthouse?" asked Officer Friedman.

"No one saw me. I waited an hour and then came home," said Encyclopedia.

"He was out at the lighthouse, but no one saw him!" jeered Bugs. "Boy, if I couldn't think up a better alibi, I'd eat my head!"

"Your mouth is big enough," snapped Sally. "What were you doing on the beach anyway?"

Bugs strutted in the doorway. "I was getting this suntan," he said. "Meet the next Mr. Junior Idaville."

He lifted his arm and made a muscle.

"A suntan makes your muscles stand out better," he went on. "You can't just lie down to bake. You've got to keep turning so you don't burn too much on one side."

Encyclopedia had to agree that Bugs had done a good job of tanning himself. There wasn't a spot that was too light or too dark on his arms, legs, or body.

"I'll bet this little crook hid my wristwatch right here," said Bugs. "He's planning to sell it when things cool down."

"Search the place," Encyclopedia invited. "You won't find your wristwatch."

"Oh, yeah?" sneered Bugs.

He began searching the shelves at the back of the garage.

"Getting a suntan is a real art," he boasted. "I'd been tanning myself on the beach three hours when those two big guys jumped me. One more hour and I'd have been ready to walk off with the Mr. Junior Idaville title."

As he talked, his smoothly tanned hands and wrists dipped into the boxes on the top shelf. Suddenly his face lighted up. He pulled out a wristwatch.

"Here it is!" he cried. "My own mother gave it to me. I treasure it above life itself!"

He glared at Encyclopedia and added, "You dirty little thief!"

"Stop acting, Bugs," said Encyclopedia calmly. "You're only trying to get even. It won't work. Your wristwatch was never stolen."

WHAT WAS
ENCYCLOPEDIA'S PROOF?

(Turn to page 75 for the solution to The Case of Bugs Meany's Revenge.)

The Case of
the Cave Drawings

Elmer Evans came into the Brown Detective Agency. He was breathing.

Elmer never breathed if he didn't have to. Although only nine, he could hold his breath for two minutes and fifty seconds.

Every day Elmer tried to keep from breathing another second. He went around with his lips pressed together, his eyes popping, and his face ready to bust.

"You're looking fine," Encyclopedia greeted him. "Is something wrong?"

"Plenty," answered Elmer. "Who is the champion breath-holder around these parts?"

"You," said Encyclopedia.

"That's what I thought," said Elmer. He

drew a long, heavy breath. "Until yester-day."

"Somebody locked his lungs for longer than two minutes and fifty seconds?" asked Encyclopedia. "Who?"

"Wilford Wiggins," said Elmer. "He must have swallowed a cork."

Wilford Wiggins was a high-school drop-out with more get-rich-quick ideas than Texans around a spot of oil.

"What's Wilford up to now?" asked Encyclopedia.

"Down to," corrected Elmer. "He climbed down that hole in the old bear cave yesterday. So I had to try, too."

"Good grief!" exclaimed Encyclopedia. "Children are supposed to stay away from the bear cave. The hole is dangerous. Poisonous gases have built up in it. You could have died!"

"I held my breath," said Elmer.

"Did you reach bottom?"

"Missed," said Elmer glumly. "I let my-self down with a clothes line. After a min-ute I hadn't reached bottom. So I pulled myself back up before I ran out of breath. But Wilford said he made it."

"How do you know he did?" demanded Encyclopedia.

"Wilford has called a secret meeting for five o'clock at the cave," said Elmer. "He's going to tell all the kids what he found in the hole. He says he'll make us all rich."

"Wilford didn't invite me to the meeting," said Encyclopedia pointedly.

"He's probably still sore at you," said Elmer. "He'll never forget how you ruined his sale of Hercules Strength Tonic last month."

"The stuff was nothing but sugar water," muttered Encyclopedia. "I think I'll go to the meeting with you."

The bear cave was a mile outside the town line. When Encyclopedia and Elmer arrived, a crowd of boys and girls had already gathered to hear Wilford.

Wilford raised his hands and called for quiet.

"Do you kids know what's inside this cave?" he asked.

"Sure we know," said Bugs Meany. "A lot of rock and a hole in the floor that goes down to China."

Wilford laughed. "That hole is filled with

Wilford raised his hands and called for quiet.

gases that can kill you," he said. "Nobody but me ever dared go down."

"How come you didn't get gassed to death?" asked Charlie Stewart.

"Because I breathed through air tanks, the same kind skin divers use," replied Wilford.

"Air tanks!" whispered Elmer gleefully. "Then I'm still the champion breath-holder!"

"You want to know what I found at the bottom of that hole?" cried Wilford. "Another cave, bigger than the one on top. On the walls were drawings—done by cavemen!"

A thrill of excitement ran through the children.

"We have to keep this a secret, see?" said Wilford. "If some smart grownup hears what's down that hole, he'll buy this land in a hurry. He'll clean up charging tourists and art lovers three dollars a ticket to see those caveman drawings!"

The children nodded in agreement. There was a fortune in it!

"I can rent this land," said Wilford. "I have the money. But I need a little more cash to dig open a better way to get to the lower cave than by the hole."

"I figured you'd put the touch on us," grumbled Rocky Graham, one of Bugs Meany's Tigers.

"Scram, kid," muttered Wilford. To the other children he said cheerfully, "I'm going to let each and every one of you buy a piece of this business for five dollars. We'll all be partners."

"How do we know those walls have caveman drawings on them?" asked Benny Breslin.

"After I discovered those priceless caveman drawings, I went home and got my camera," said Wilford. "I took pictures with a flashgun."

He passed out three photographs.

The first photograph was of a woolly rhinoceros. The second was of cavemen attacking a dinosaur. The third was of a charging mammoth.

"There's the proof!" shouted Wilford. "This attraction will be bigger than Yellowstone Park. For five bucks you'll all get a share of every ticket sold. So go home and get your money. But remember! Don't breathe a word of this great discovery to anyone. Not even your mother!"

"Maybe I spoke too quick, Wilford," Rocky Graham apologized. "I'm sorry. I've got ten dollars saved. Can I buy two shares?"

"Sure, sure, kid," said Wilford grandly. "I don't have the heart to keep anybody from a big money-making deal like this."

Rocky and the other Tigers raced for their bikes. They chattered about using the club treasury to buy all the shares themselves.

Encyclopedia watched the Tigers pedal away. Then he told the rest of the children to hold onto their money.

"No caveman drew those pictures," he said.

HOW DID ENCYCLOPEDIA KNOW?

(Turn to page 76 for the solution to The Case of the Cave Drawings.)

 WANTED

The Case of
the Wanted Man

"I'm never going to shave."

Encyclopedia glanced up from his book. Standing in the door of the Brown Detective Agency was six-year-old Bryan Horton.

"You're never going to shave?" asked Encyclopedia, pretending to be serious. "But you must. Beards aren't allowed in second grade."

"Shaving takes too much time," said Bryan. "When I grow up and get my picture taken, I'll just pull off my beard."

"Ouch!" said Encyclopedia.

Bryan looked surprised. "Does it hurt to pull off your beard?"

"Only around the face," answered Encyclopedia.

"The man didn't hurt himself," said Bryan. "He was smiling."

"What man?" asked Encyclopedia.

"The man who pulled off his beard to have his picture taken," said Bryan impatiently. "What kind of detective are you?"

Talking with a boy of six wasn't always easy, decided Encyclopedia. He started over. "Do you need help?"

"That's why I'm here, isn't it?" said Bryan. "I want you to read the big words under the man's picture. It's hanging in the post office. Boy, he must be famous."

"Famous?" yelped Encyclopedia. "He's a wanted man. Only dangerous crooks have their pictures hanging in the post office!"

Encyclopedia rolled out his bike. He put Bryan on the crossbar and rode swiftly to the post office.

"After I saw the man pull off his beard, my Mom took me with her to mail a package," said Bryan. "She got awful sore when I played with the stamp machine. She made me stand over there."

He pointed to a bulletin board on the post office wall. A bunch of small posters were tacked to one corner.

"That's him," said Bryan. "The one on top."

Encyclopedia saw two photographs of a clean-shaven young man. One showed him full-faced, the other from the side. There were small pictures of each of his ten fingerprints and a line of heavy type: "WANTED FOR ARMED HOLDUP."

Encyclopedia read further: "William Matson, alias Billy, Bill, The Kid." Below this was smaller type giving Matson's long criminal record.

"Wow! This is a case for Dad," exclaimed Encyclopedia.

He telephoned his father at once. Then he questioned Bryan.

He learned that Bryan now lived at the Beach Motel, which his father had just bought. That morning Bryan had seen the wanted man, William Matson, get into his car, pull off his beard, and drive away.

"He wasn't going to have his picture taken," explained Encyclopedia. "This photograph was taken three years ago.

Bryan had seen the wanted man get into his car,
pull off his beard, and drive away.

See, there's the date. The beard was fake. He wore it so nobody would know him."

When Chief Brown arrived at the post office, Encyclopedia repeated what he had learned.

"Matson must not have seen Bryan," said Chief Brown. "Otherwise, he would not have risked taking off his beard. It probably itched. So he took it off as soon as he could."

"Do you think he'll come back to the motel?" asked Encyclopedia.

"Little chance of that," replied Chief Brown. "But perhaps he left a clue in his room that will tell us where he is going."

Chief Brown returned to the patrol car. Encyclopedia did not see him again till dinner.

Chief Brown finished his barley soup before bringing up the case.

"William Matson spent a week at the Beach Motel under the name Bill Martin. He paid his bill and drove to the airport."

"How did you find that out, Dad?"

"Bryan's father writes down the license plate number of everyone who stops at his motel," said Chief Brown. "Matson's license began with an E, the letter given to all rented cars in the state. We traced the car to the airport branch of Easy Car Rental Service."

"Did Matson get on a plane?" asked Encyclopedia.

"Very likely," said Chief Brown. "But he uses so many different names that he can't be traced as a passenger."

Chief Brown took a slip of paper from his pocket before continuing.

"Bryan's father overheard Matson talking on the pay telephone," said Chief Brown. "He didn't hear much except the words, 'ticket to Moscow.' Matson wrote several places on a pad in his room. He forgot that his pencil dug into the sheet beneath. I had the writing brought out."

Chief Brown passed the paper to Encyclopedia. On it was written: Moscow, Odessa, London, Paris, Palestine, Athens.

"Matson has been mixed up in jewelry thefts," said Chief Brown. "He must have hidden in Idaville till he thought it was safe to move his loot. That list must be of places where he hopes to sell the stolen jewels."

Mrs. Brown picked up the piece of paper. She studied it for a long moment.

"It's a strange list," she said. "Two cities

in Russia—Moscow and Odessa. Then look here. London is in England, Paris is in France, and Athens is in Greece. But he didn't list any city in Palestine."

"That struck me as odd, too," said Chief Brown. "I want Leroy to examine the list before I call Washington. I don't want the F.B.I. to check planes landing overseas for nothing."

Encyclopedia had closed his eyes. He was doing his deepest thinking.

"Matson didn't fly across the ocean," he said. "You'll find him in—"

WHERE?

*(Turn to page 77 for the solution to
The Case of the Wanted Man.)*

The Case of
the Angry Cook

Encyclopedia and Sally were in downtown Idaville when they saw a very short sailor sneaking in and out of doorways.

As he drew closer, the detectives recognized Cicero Sturgess, Idaville's greatest child actor.

"Why should Cicero dress as a sailor?" said Sally. "He hates boats with all his heart and stomach."

Encyclopedia could only agree. After getting seasick on a submarine sandwich last year, Cicero had thrown a curse upon the ships of the world.

"He probably is in a new play," said Sally as an afterthought. "The sailor suit must be his costume."

"He's acting strangely," said Encyclopedia. "Something has scared the tar out of him."

Cicero spied the partners. He ducked into a doorway and beckoned to them desperately. The moment they came within reach, he threw himself upon Encyclopedia.

"A cazy crook just tried to kill me!" he wailed.

"What kind of crook?" asked Encyclopedia.

"I mean, a *crazy cook*," said Cicero.

"A cook tried to poison you?" exclaimed Sally.

"He tried to cut my head off—*swsssht!*" said Cicero, slicing the air like one of the three musketeers. "He chased me with a knife big enough to chop down Grant's Tomb."

Cicero threw up his arms and moaned, "I never should have cursed the ships of the world." Then, remembering he was not on stage, he related what had happened to him.

When the destroyer *John Adams* had docked at Idaville last night, he had decided to study how real seamen behaved.

"I'm going to be in a play about the Navy," he said. "So I took all my money, ten dollars, and followed the sailors around. Mostly they went into restaurants. I stuffed in hamburgers and listened to them talk all morning. When I got to The Beefy Burger Palace, I was nearly broke."

"You ate ten dollars' worth of hamburgers in one morning?" cried Sally.

"Heavens, no!" said Cicero. "It cost me three dollars to rent this uniform and four dollars more to have it shortened."

"The Beefy Burger Palace," said Encyclopedia. "Is that where you ran into the cutthroat cook?"

"Yes, not five minutes ago," said Cicero. "After I paid my check, I had only two cents left. It wasn't enough for a tip. I was so ashamed! I crawled out."

"Crawled?" said Sally. "On your hands and knees?"

"It was the fastest way," said Cicero. "As I turned to leave, I bumped into a big sailor standing right behind me. I fell down and crawled out the door."

"That's when the cook came at you?" asked Encyclopedia.

"Not quite," answered Cicero. "I'd

walked a block when I heard sounds like a truck backfiring. The next thing I knew, the cook was running after me. He was waving his knife and screaming, 'I fix you good!' I didn't argue. I took off.''

"What did the sailor look like?" asked Encyclopedia. "The one you bumped into?"

"I didn't see his face," said Cicero. "Anyway, what has *he* got to do with it?"

"I don't know—yet," said Encyclopedia. "Wait here."

Leaving Cicero in the doorway, Encyclopedia and Sally went to The Beefy Burger Palace on Fourth Street. Inside the little restaurant Officer Webb was talking with a big sailor and a cook.

"We didn't get here a second too soon," said Encyclopedia.

"I've never been in here before in my life," the sailor was telling Officer Webb. "I didn't try to pull a stickup. There must be three hundred sailors in town today. He's made a mistake."

"No mistake!" shouted the cook. "You had a partner—a little guy. I should have known. They don't let shrimps like him into the United States Navy!"

The cook was running after Cicero. He was waving his knife and screaming, "I fix you good!"

"My gosh," whispered Sally. "I think he's talking about Cicero!"

"The little guy—he looked like a kid—sat right here at the counter," said the cook. "When the place was empty, he got up and paid. He acted funny."

"Funny?" questioned Officer Webb.

"Sort of nervous," said the cook. "He turned to go and bumped into his partner here and fell down. While I was watching the little guy crawl out the door, this big one pulled a gun. See how they worked it? Slick!"

"Then what did you do?" said Officer Webb.

"This big fellow told me to hand over all my money. Instead, I dived behind the counter. He fired a few shots, got scared, and beat it."

"You kept him in sight while you gave chase?"

"Well, not quite," said the cook. "When I got outside, I saw the little shrimp first. He took off faster than a rabbit. I figured the two of them had split up. So I doubled back to look for the big fellow. I saw him on Third Street. That's when I hollered to you, officer."

"I tell you he's made a mistake," protested the big sailor. "Look, officer. When you brought me back here, did I fight? No! Did I have a gun? No! So how many times do I have to say it? You've got the wrong man!"

"He must have thrown the gun away," growled the cook.

"I believe the big sailor," Sally whispered to Encyclopedia. "The cook made a mistake."

"What makes you so certain?"

"He's not very smart if he thinks Cicero had a hand in a stickup!"

"The cook didn't make a mistake. Cicero brought suspicion upon himself," replied Encyclopedia. "The big sailor is guilty!"

HOW DID ENCYCLOPEDIA KNOW?

(Turn to page 78 for the solution to
The Case of the Angry Cook.)

The Case of
the Missing Ring

Because of Idaville's wonderful police record, Chief Brown was often asked to solve cases in other towns.

One evening he received a call to help the police of Ocean City. He took Encyclopedia with him.

"What is the case all about?" asked Encyclopedia, getting into the car beside his father.

"A ring is missing," answered Chief Brown. "Two masked men broke into the home of Mr. James Bevan last night. But no one, including Mr. Bevan, is sure the ring was stolen."

"How come?" said Encyclopedia.

"I didn't get all the facts over the telephone," replied Chief Brown. "But the mystery has to do with Mr. Bevan himself. He lost his memory. He left a note, but he doesn't remember writing it."

Encyclopedia had never come up against anything like *that*. The half hour's drive seemed to take all night.

At last his father slowed the car and parked before a large house.

Chief Moore of the Ocean City police department appeared at the door.

"I'm glad you could come," he said. "This case has me going around in circles."

After shaking hands, he led Encyclopedia and his father into the study.

"The house belongs to Mr. James Bevan," he said. "The theft of the ring—if there was a theft—took place last night."

"What does the ring look like?" asked Chief Brown.

"It's a diamond ring," said Chief Moore. "It belonged to King Louis XIV of France. It's worth a fortune!"

Chief Moore pointed to a tiny glass box which lay on the desk beside a typewriter.

"Mr. Bevan kept the ring in the glass box to admire it," he said. "It was too small to fit his finger."

Then, for the next few minutes he told Chief Brown and Encyclopedia what he knew about the case. The facts were:

On the night of the theft, Mrs. Bevan had gone to a movie. Mr. Bevan had stayed home, for he needed a cane to get around and seldom went out.

About midnight the doorbell rang. Mr. Bevan, who was alone in the house, opened the door. Two masked men pushed their way inside. They demanded to know where the diamond ring was kept.

Mr. Bevan told them it was upstairs in his wife's jewelry case. He wanted time to hide the ring. As the men started upstairs, one of them hit him on the head with a gun.

"That's all Mr. Bevan can tell me," said Chief Moore. "I spoke with him this morning in the hospital. He can't remember a thing that happened between the time he was hit and the moment he woke up in the hospital."

"Did the two thieves steal Mrs. Bevan's jewels?" asked Chief Brown.

"Yes, but Mrs. Bevan says the whole lot isn't worth half of the diamond ring."

"Is there any clue to prove that Mr.

Bevan, after he was hit on the head, hid the diamond ring so the thieves couldn't find it?" said Chief Brown.

"This typewritten note," said Chief Moore, taking a sheet of paper from his pocket. He showed it to Chief Brown and Encyclopedia. It read:

"Two men tried to steal the diamond ring. They hunted all over the house, raving about like madmen. They even split open the cat! When all failed, they beat me, but I didn't tell and so they hunted a little while longer. I may be dying. I hid the ring in the vane."

"If I understand the case so far," said Chief Brown, "Mr. Bevan wrote the note to his wife while the thieves searched the house. He feared he was dying from the beating and might not live to tell where he hid the diamond."

"Correct," said Chief Moore. "He must have put the note in a drawer of the desk after the thieves had searched it. Now he can't remember anything. He can't recall hiding the diamond ring or typing the note."

"Who found him?" asked Chief Brown.

"His wife—when she returned from the movie," said Chief Brown. "He was lying on the floor near the desk."

"Did you look for the ring in the vane?" asked Chief Brown. "The note says he hid it there."

"The only vane Mr. Bevan knows of is the weather vane on the roof," said Chief Moore. "I took it down. The ring wasn't inside it."

"What about the cat?"

"That part is the biggest mystery," said Chief Moore. "Why should thieves split open a cat, unless they thought the poor animal had swallowed the ring?"

"Did you find its body?" asked Chief Brown.

"No," answered Chief Moore. "Mr. Bevan never owned a cat. I suppose a cat must have got into the house somehow, and the thieves took no chances. They looked into everything. Why, they tore the house apart. Come with me."

He led Encyclopedia and Chief Brown down to the basement. It was in ruins. Everything was overturned. A large wooden barrel, or vat, had been split open. Wine from it spilled over the floor.

Mrs. Bevan returned and found him lying on the floor near the desk.

"This morning the rest of the house looked as bad," said Chief Moore. "Mrs. Bevan worked all day with the help of neighbors straightening up."

"Perhaps the thieves did find the diamond ring," said Chief Brown. "They might have typed the note themselves to throw us off their trail."

"No, they didn't, Dad," whispered Encyclopedia. "The diamond ring is hidden in—"

WHERE?

(Turn to page 79 for the solution to The Case of the Missing Ring.)

The Case of
the Money-Changer

Hector Conklin pushed a wheelbarrow full of old socks into the Brown Detective Agency. The socks clinked.

He put twenty-five cents on the gasoline can beside Encyclopedia. "I want to hire you in a hurry," he said.

"What's the problem?" asked Encyclopedia.

"I need change," said Hector. He waved toward the socks. "They're filled with pennies. I was on my way to put them in the bank when Red Slattery saw me. I had to pull in here."

"Oh," said Encyclopedia, understanding.

Red Slattery was a tough teenager. He went from neighborhood to neighborhood asking children to change a quarter for him. When he got *all* their money, he forgot to give them his quarter.

"If Red finds out what's in the socks, I'm ruined," wailed Hector. "The pennies are my life's savings. I've got to give Red the slip!"

Encyclopedia considered the case.

He could make change for Hector and let him sneak through the house and out by the back door. But then *he* would be stuck with Red Slattery and a wheelbarrow full of pennies!

Hector peeked out the garage door. "Red's down the block. He's waiting for me to come out. I'm trapped like a dog!"

"Don't panic," said Encyclopedia, as much to himself as to Hector.

"You've got to get me out of here, quick!" cried Hector. "I don't dare refuse to make change for Red. No one does. Bugs Meany tried last week and you know what happened."

"I k-know," said Encyclopedia unsteadily. "Bugs told Red to put a hat in his mouth. So Red emptied Bugs's pockets and threw him into Mill Creek."

"Somebody ought to tell a grownup about what Red is doing. But all the kids are scared stiff—like me," said Hector disgustedly.

"That's the answer!" exclaimed Encyclopedia. "We've got to have a grownup catch Red in the act! How much money is in the socks?"

"Fifteen dollars and eight cents," answered Hector. "Red will get it all if we don't move fast."

"We will," said Encyclopedia. "Follow me."

He led Hector through the house, out the back door, across Mr. Colby's yard, and to Mr. Link's back door.

Mr. Link was an artist and worked at home. He was also a coin collector.

Encyclopedia told him about Red Slattery. Mr. Link agreed to watch Red's money-changing trick.

Encyclopedia asked for a loan of seven dollars and nineteen cents. Hector would have to have money when Red asked for change, he explained.

"We'll need one five-dollar bill, a one-dollar bill, one half-dollar, one quarter, four dimes, and four pennies," said the boy sleuth.

After Mr. Link had left the living room to fetch the money, Hector said, "We could mark the bills. Then Red couldn't deny he took the money."

"No, Red might notice the marks and be scared off," said Encyclopedia. "We'll copy the numbers of the bills and dates of the coins on a sheet of paper."

Mr. Link returned with the money. Encyclopedia copied the numbers and the dates. Then he had Hector empty his pockets. Mr. Link saw that Hector had no money of his own to help make change for Red.

"Now return to the garage the way we came," Encyclopedia told Hector, "and then come back here by the sidewalk. Be sure you stop right in front of the house. Mr. Link must be able to see and hear everything Red says and does."

Hector grabbed the seven dollars and nineteen cents and raced out Mr. Link's back door. A minute later Encyclopedia saw him approaching on the sidewalk.

Red's voice called, "Hey, kid! Wait a second."

Hector stopped in front of Mr. Link's house.

"I need some change," said Red, coming up.

"Glad to help," said Hector. He took out Mr. Link's money. "What do you want change for?"

At that moment Encyclopedia and Mr. Link took their gaze from the window. Mrs. Link had entered the room. "It's time for lunch," she said to Mr. Link.

"In a moment, dear," replied Mr. Link. "In a moment!"

He and Encyclopedia turned from Mrs. Link and looked outside again. Red was walking away, grinning.

"We missed it!" thought Encyclopedia.

Mr. Link ran from the house. "Hold it, son," he shouted.

Red stopped and turned around uneasily.

"Did you just take money from this boy?" demanded Mr. Link.

"I didn't *take* anything," retorted Red. "I got change."

"Glad to help," said Hector. "What do
you want change for?"

"Let's see the money he gave you," said Mr. Link.

Red glared. "I don't have to show you anything, or tell you anything," he said. "You're no cop. I know my rights!"

"If I made change for you, where's the money you gave me?" said Hector. He pulled his pockets inside out. "I don't have a cent."

Red pointed to a drain in the gutter near Hector.

"You dropped all the money I gave you down the drain, remember?" he said. "Clumsy of you, kid."

Mr. Link turned to Encyclopedia worriedly.

"That could have happened while we both looked at my wife," he said to Encyclopedia. "It will be Red's word against Hector's. Without using force to search Red, we can't prove he stole the seven dollars and nineteen cents."

"Oh, yes we can!" said Encyclopedia.

HOW?

(Turn to page 80 for the solution to The Case of the Money-Changer.)

The Case of
the Falling Woman

Encyclopedia was sitting in the Kimball living room after dinner when Sally suddenly clutched his arm.

"Listen," she whispered. "Someone is outside the house."

Encyclopedia also heard the noise. He looked at the window. Since it was dark outside and light inside, the glass of the window acted as a mirror. He saw only the reflection of the living room.

"It could be one of those peeping Toms!" said Sally. "I'll fix him." She reached for a heavy floor lamp.

"Don't try it," warned Encyclopedia. "He may be dangerous. Make believe you're going to the bookcase. Switch off the lights as you pass the door."

Sally did not understand. Nevertheless, she got up and switched off the lights.

Now the room was darker than the moonlit outdoors. Encyclopedia could see through the window.

A boy was standing under a sycamore tree. He held a camera.

"It's Scott Curtis," said Encyclopedia, opening the window.

Sally was horrified. "I nearly crowned him with a floor lamp!"

"You can catch a terrible headache snooping under the sycamores, Scott," called Encyclopedia. "Come inside."

"I wasn't snooping," said Scott as he entered the house. "I saw you two sitting on the sofa. I thought you'd make a nice picture. I was going to call it 'Sitting at Sally's.' "

"You mean *lying* at Sally's!" snapped Sally. "What were you *really* doing in the back yard with a camera?"

"I was looking for things to photograph," said Scott. "Wednesday is the Junior Photography Show. First prize is a three-speed bicycle."

"Gosh, I forgot about the show. I'm sorry for what I said," Sally apologized. "I hope you win the bicycle."

"The best I can do is the lady's folding umbrella," said Scott. "That's second prize. Winthrop Ledbetter will win the bicycle."

"Winthrop always wins," grumbled Sally.

"By hook or by crook," added Scott.

"Every kid in the neighborhood knows how Winthrop won the boys' championships at tennis, golf, and riflery last year," said Sally. "He cheated."

"I'm sorry I didn't report him," said Encyclopedia, remembering. Whenever Winthrop had fallen behind in a match, a friend had come to the rescue. The friend had screamed bird calls from hiding just as Winthrop's opponent was serving, putting, or shooting.

"It was cuckoos at the courts, goshawks at the greens, and road runners at the range," recalled Encyclopedia. "The friend had style."

"Winthrop will try anything to win," said Scott. "I want to hire you on Wednesday to be . . . well, to be a kind of watchdog."

"Bird dog, you mean," said Encyclopedia, and agreed to take the case.

On Wednesday, Encyclopedia and Sally biked to the American Legion Hall. The walls were hung with photographs taken by the young cameramen of Idaville.

Scott Curtis had four pictures in the show. Encyclopedia was thinking that Scott would be hard to beat when Sally tugged at his sleeve.

"Winthrop has only one picture," she said. "But wait till you see it!"

Encyclopedia blinked as he gazed upon Winthrop's photograph.

It showed a teenage girl touching a flaming match to a Christmas candle. Beside the candle stood a pile of gifts which was lighted by two table lamps.

What made the picture amazing, however, was the second figure. It was a woman. She could be seen falling outside the large window behind the teenage girl.

The picture was titled "Christmas Miracle." Beside it was pinned a white card on which was written:

This photograph was taken December 16, at 9:30 P.M., by Winthrop Ledbetter,

*She could be seen falling outside the large window
behind the teenage girl.*

age 11, in the living room of his parents' apartment. At the moment Winthrop snapped the picture of his teenage sister Mary, Miss Abigail Greer was toppling from the apartment house roof one story above. Miss Greer's falling body made this startling background for a photograph that was meant to be used as the Ledbetter family's Christmas card.

Miss Greer later said she had lost her footing in the storm winds that reached 40 miles an hour. By a miracle, she landed on an awning and suffered only a broken leg.

The picture was taken with a Crown camera and flashgun.

Encyclopedia said slowly, "There's something wrong in that picture. . . ."

"Find out what it is, but hurry!" said Sally. "Here come the judges."

Three men were marching toward Winthrop's photograph. One of the men carried a blue ribbon.

"They're going to give Winthrop first prize—and the bicycle!" said Sally. "Encyclopedia, you've got to tell them the picture is nothing but a fake! It is . . . isn't it?"

Encyclopedia didn't seem to be listen-

ing. He was gazing intently at the picture.
Suddenly he smiled.

"It's a fake, all right," he said. "Winthrop couldn't have snapped that picture without a real miracle!"

HOW DID ENCYCLOPEDIA KNOW?

*(Turn to page 81 for the solution to
The Case of the Falling Woman.)*

The Case of
the Red Boat

"All set for the fish, son?" asked Chief Brown.

Encyclopedia lifted his fishing pole. "All set," he answered smiling.

He didn't really feel like smiling. He felt like asking questions. He had seen his father slip a gun into the lunchbox.

During the drive to the docks, Encyclopedia finally got up courage to ask, "Are we really going fishing, Dad?"

"Of course," replied Chief Brown. "Why do you ask?"

"You brought a gun?" said Encyclopedia.

"Oh . . ." said Chief Brown. "You saw it?

Well, I don't expect we'll meet trouble. I brought it along just in case."

"In case of what?"

"Do you remember the robbery four days ago down in the islands?" Chief Brown said.

"Two armed men robbed one of the millionaire's homes," said Encyclopedia. "They got away with three hundred thousand dollars' worth of jewels and furs."

"The robbers escaped by motorboat," said Chief Brown.

"That was four days ago. You don't think they're still at sea!" exclaimed Encyclopedia.

"It's possible," said Chief Brown. "About the time the robbers made their escape, a storm broke. The rains lasted only an hour or so. But there have been high winds until today."

"Do you believe the winds blew the robbers' boat out to sea?" asked Encyclopedia.

"The robbers could still be at sea, out of gas and drifting," said Chief Brown. "But let's forget about them. Let's think about fish."

At the docks, Encyclopedia helped his

father unload the car. They bought ice and bait at the little store by the gas pumps. When everything was aboard, Chief Brown started the motor.

"Cast off," he called.

Encyclopedia undid the lines. The boat was a twenty footer with an outboard motor. Chief Brown rented her three or four Sundays each summer.

"We'll try our luck in the ocean first," said Chief Brown. "If nothing is biting, we can come closer to shore and try for snapper and flounder."

The boat moved smoothly across the calm waters of the bay. Once in the ocean, Chief Brown speeded up. As the shore fell farther and farther behind, Encyclopedia thought of the robbers.

What if he and his father met them at sea?

The robbers were armed. Would they try to come aboard like pirates? Or would they throw the stolen jewels and furs into the ocean and say they were harmless boatmen?

According to the newspaper stories, the two robbers had worn masks. No one knew what they looked like. As it had been dark, no one could be sure of what their boat looked like—only that it was not white.

Chief Brown slowed the motor. He handed Encyclopedia a fishing rod. "Time to try our luck," he said.

The fish were biting. Father and son had landed ten beauties when Chief Brown suddenly put aside his rod. For several minutes he looked through field glasses at a small red boat in the distance.

Then he called the Coast Guard on the ship-to-shore radio.

Within forty minutes a Coast Guard cutter came alongside. It carried a big gun on the front deck.

Chief Brown greeted the captain. "I think that's the one we've been looking for," he said, pointing to the red boat. "I would have moved closer, but my son is with me."

"Better drop anchor and come aboard," said the captain. "This will be the safest place if there is shooting."

Chief Brown put over the anchor. He and Encyclopedia climbed aboard the cutter. The captain shouted orders. The cutter headed for the small red boat.

At first the red boat seemed empty. Then

For several minutes Chief Brown looked through field glasses at a small red boat in the distance.

Encyclopedia saw a man. He came out of the tiny cabin and waved.

The cutter swung alongside. A rope ladder was dropped, and the man reached for it weakly. Three Coast Guardsmen helped him aboard.

"Thank goodness you saw us!" the man gasped, stepping onto the deck of the cutter. He took off his cap. With a handkerchief he wiped the heavy sweat from his bald head and face. "Water, please," he said. "Water!"

Water was brought. The man drank it in great gulps.

"I'm Roger Ascot," he said at last. "Ben Page and I were out for a day's fishing when the storm hit us. The waves were terrible. The radio went dead right away. Sea water got into the gas, and the engine quit."

Again he dried the sweat from his head and face with his handkerchief.

"We've been drifting four days without food and water," he went on. "We had some food in a chest, but it was washed overboard with our fishing things. Ben passed out yesterday from thirst. He's in the cabin."

Ben Page was immediately brought onto the cutter and taken below. Roger Ascot followed him.

Chief Brown climbed down the rope ladder. For a few minutes he looked carefully around the red boat.

"There's water in the gas, all right," he said. "The radio doesn't work, and I don't see any food or drinking water."

"How about guns?" said Encyclopedia. "And the stolen jewels and furs?"

"The boat is clean," said Chief Brown. "I may have made a mistake. Roger Ascot and Ben Page don't appear to be the robbers."

"Don't believe Roger Ascot's story," warned Encyclopedia. "He has the face of a liar!"

WHAT DID ENCYCLOPEDIA MEAN?

*(Turn to page 82 for the solution to
The Case of the Red Boat.)*

Solution to *The Case of the Silver Fruit Bowl*

Chief Brown's words pointed out to Encyclopedia where Mr. Holt had lied.

Chief Brown said that the silver fruit bowl "was rounded inside like a big spoon."

It would have been impossible for Mr. Holt, looking into the fruit bowl, to get a good idea of what the holdup man looked like, as he claimed.

Look into a shiny spoon. What do you see? You see yourself as in a mirror, but—*upside down!*

Shown how impossible his story was, Mr. Holt told the truth. He had made up the holdup man. He had stolen the silver dishes himself, hoping to sell them in another city and keep all the money.

Solution to *The Case of the Dwarf's Beard*

Bugs claimed he had burned the candle in the clubhouse with the door open.

Further, he said he had not touched the candle after placing it on the orange crate.

But the dwarf faced the door, from where the breeze came. And "all the drippings" of the melted wax were on the *front* of the dwarf.

Bugs had never noticed that candles drip on the side away from a breeze.

If Bugs had been telling the truth, the drippings would have spilled down the dwarf's *back!*

Caught lying, he returned the candles to Gary.

Solution to *The Case of Bugs Meany's Revenge*

Bugs said he had been tanning himself "for three hours" when the two big men "took the watch right off my wrist."

Yet "there wasn't a spot" on Bugs "that was too light or too dark on his arms, legs, or body." Further, his hands and *wrists* were "smoothly tanned."

Had Bugs really been robbed as he claimed, there would have been a white, untanned mark around his wrist where the watch had been worn for three hours in the sun!

Bugs confessed. He had sent Encyclopedia on a wild-goose chase with the telephone call. Then Duke Kelly, one of his Tigers, had slipped into the Brown garage and hidden the watch in the box for Bugs to find.

Solution to *The Case of the Cave Drawings*

Encyclopedia knew that Wilford Wiggins had drawn the cave pictures himself and then photographed them.

One of the photographs which Wilford passed around showed a drawing of "cavemen attacking a dinosaur." That was Wilford's mistake!

Human beings did not live on earth at the same time that the dinosaurs did.

The first man did not appear until millions of years after the last dinosaur had died.

Since the cavemen artists did not even know that dinosaurs ever lived, they could not have known what a dinosaur looked like!

Because of Encyclopedia's sharp eye, Wilford went out of the cave business.

 WANTED

Solution to *The Case of the Wanted Man*

Encyclopedia saw what was wrong—the word "Palestine."

Palestine is the old name for Israel. If William Matson were going there, he would have written Israel.

So Encyclopedia knew the list was not what it seemed at first glance—names of foreign places.

He told his father that Matson had flown to Texas.

And that is where the police arrested him—in a motel in Palestine, Texas.

Encyclopedia remembered that Moscow, Odessa, London, Paris, Athens, and Palestine are names of towns in Texas!

Solution to *The Case of the Angry Cook*

The big sailor gave himself away with one word.

After Encyclopedia and Sally arrived at The Beefy Burger Palace, what did the big sailor say to Officer Webb?

He said, "I've never been in here before in my life."

Later, what did he say?

He said, "Look, officer. When you brought me back here, did I fight?"

The word "back" was his slip.

If he really had never been in The Beefy Burger Palace before, he could not have been brought *back* to it!

Solution to *The Case of the Missing Ring*

Encyclopedia knew that Mr. Bevan had typed the word "cat" in his note by mistake.

Only the wood barrel, also called a vat, in the basement had been "split open." This was the clue.

The boy detective did not believe that Mr. Bevan, after being hit on the head, and beaten up, could have typed the note without making a mistake.

Mr. Bevan's mistake, Encyclopedia saw, was that he had struck the letter "v" whenever he had meant to strike the letter "c." These letters are next to each other on a typewriter keyboard.

So Mr. Bevan had typed "cat" instead of "vat," "raving" instead of "racing." And when he wrote where he had hidden the ring, he had typed "vane" instead of "cane."

Thanks to Encyclopedia, the ring was found in Mr. Bevan's cane!

Solution to *The Case of the Money-Changer*

Red knew Mr. Link would not search him by force. So Red didn't have to tell how much change he had asked for and received.

But Red made one mistake. He *admitted* he had got change.

Encyclopedia, however, had made sure Hector couldn't give Red any change at all! Hector had seven dollars and nineteen cents made up of one five-dollar bill, a one-dollar bill, one half dollar, one quarter, four dimes, and four pennies.

With that in his pocket, Hector couldn't have made change for *any* coin or bill!

Outsmarted by Encyclopedia, Red returned the seven dollars and nineteen cents. And he quit stealing from children rather than go to court.

Solution to *The Case of the Falling Woman*

As the winds of "40 miles an hour" would have blown out the match and candle, "the large window" behind Winthrop's sister must have been closed.

Further, the room was lighted by "two table lamps" and the flashgun of the camera, while outside it was night.

Thus the window should have acted as a mirror. It should have mirrored what was in the room.

Yet the falling woman could be seen *through* the window. Impossible!

Winthrop admitted the picture was faked. He had put it together in his darkroom.

So first prize—the blue ribbon and bicycle—was given to Scott.

Solution to *The Case of the Red Boat*

Roger Ascot said he and Ben Page had been without drinking water for four days.

Yet when he came aboard the Coast Guard cutter, he made a mistake—and Encyclopedia caught it right away. Roger Ascot wiped the sweat off his head and face.

After four days without a drink, Roger Ascot's body would have been dried out. He couldn't have sweated one drop!

Trapped by his lie, Roger Ascot confessed.

When he and Ben Page saw the Coast Guard cutter, they threw everything overboard—the stolen jewels and furs and their guns. To help their story of being two fishermen caught in a sudden storm, they threw their food and water overboard, too.

Then they made believe they were weak from hunger and thirst.

ABOUT THE AUTHOR

Since the publication of the first *Encyclopedia Brown* book in 1963, DONALD J. SOBOL has written roughly one book a year. In 1967, at a Children's Book Fair, he explained, "I began writing children's mysteries because the mystery element was really very small in the so-called mysteries that were written for children and I felt that this was a shame." In 1976, the *Encyclopedia Brown* series was the recipient of a special 1976 Edgar Allan Poe Award, presented by the Mystery Writers of America in recognition of these books as the first mysteries that millions of children read. In addition to the *Encyclopedia Brown* series, Mr. Sobol has authored over twenty books for young readers. A native of New York, he now lives in Florida with his wife and children. He has been a free-lance writer for eighteen years.

SKYLARK BOOKS

A series of enchanting, award-winning paperback books by celebrated authors, carefully selected to appeal to the 8–12 year old and designed to develop lifetime readers.

☐ 15019 **Abel's Island** by William Steig   **$1.75**
    A lovable mouse, a furious storm, a lonely island.

☐ 15002 **Big Red** by Jim Kjelgaard   **$1.95**
    Story of Danny and champion Irish setter, Big Red.

☐ 15015 **Jacob Two-Two Meets The Hooded Fang**   **$1.50**
    by Mordecai Richler
    Poor Jacob Two-Two, only two plus two plus two
    and a prisoner of the Hooded Fang.

☐ 15005 **Tuck Everlasting** by Natalie Babbitt   **$1.75**
    The Tuck family have unwittingly drunk from a spring
    of life.

☐ 15001 **A Dream For Addie** by Gail Rock   **$1.50**
    An Addie Mills Story
    From her unexpected friendship with an actress,
    Addie learns her dreams are worth holding onto.

Encyclopedia Brown—Donald Sobol
He's earned this nickname because of his ability to solve the mysteries in Idaville. The author gives the reader a chance to solve the case by presenting the solution—without an explanation. However, the explanations are at the back of the book.

☐ 15025 Encyclopedia Brown Boy Detective   **$1.25**
☐ 15028 Encyclopedia Brown Finds The Clues   **$1.25**
☐ 15026 Encyclopedia Brown And
    The Case Of The Secret Pitch   **$1.25**